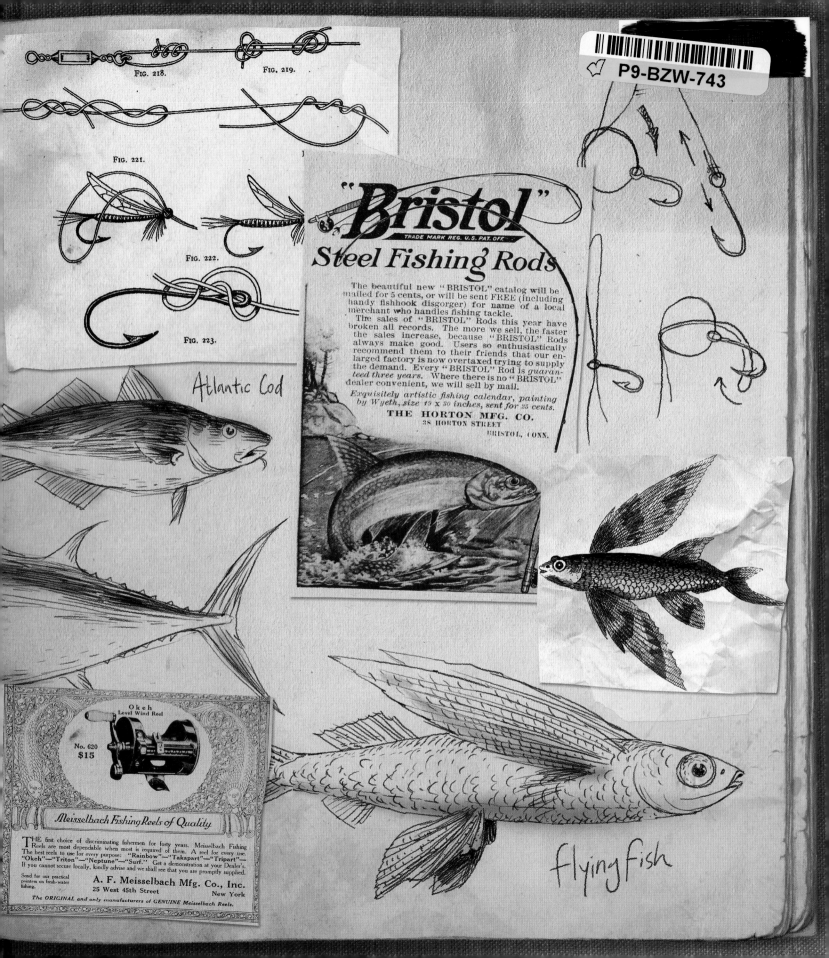

FIG. 218.

FIG. 219.

FIG. 221.

FIG. 222.

FIG. 223.

Atlantic Cod

"Bristol"
TRADE MARK REG. U.S. PAT. OFF.
Steel Fishing Rods

The beautiful new "BRISTOL" catalog will be mailed for 5 cents, or will be sent FREE (including handy fishhook disgorger) for name of a local merchant who handles fishing tackle.

The sales of "BRISTOL" Rods this year have broken all records. The more we sell, the faster the sales increase, because "BRISTOL" Rods always make good. Users so enthusiastically recommend them to their friends that our enlarged factory is now overtaxed trying to supply the demand. Every "BRISTOL" Rod is *guaranteed three years.* Where there is no "BRISTOL" dealer convenient, we will sell by mail.

Exquisitely artistic fishing calendar, painting by Wyeth, size 19 x 30 inches, sent for 25 cents.

THE HORTON MFG. CO.
38 HORTON STREET
BRISTOL, CONN.

Okeh
Level Wind Reel

No. 620
$15

Meisselbach Fishing Reels of Quality

THE first choice of discriminating fishermen for forty years. Meisselbach Fishing Reels are most dependable when most is required of them. A reel for every use. The best reels to use for every purpose: "Rainbow"—"Takapart"—"Tripart"—"Okeh"—"Triton"—"Neptune"—"Surf." Get a demonstration at your Dealer's. If you cannot secure locally, kindly advise and we shall see that you are promptly supplied.

Send for our practical pointers on fresh-water fishing.

A. F. Meisselbach Mfg. Co., Inc.
25 West 45th Street
New York

The ORIGINAL and only manufacturers of GENUINE Meisselbach Reels.

flying fish

FISHING REELS.

No. 1

No. 2

No. 3

No. 1. Henshall Reel.— (T. H. Chubb Rod Co.)
No. 2. Meek Reel.— (B. F. Meek & Sons.)
No. 3. Milam Reel.— (B. C. Milam & Son.)

Pope

Pike

Zander

Perch →

Pumpkinseed

A pocketwater teaser for swinging through riffles... hold on...

For San Juan Rainbows, it seems... #20 & #22's but better go 5X as these hogs are fullgrown!

Soft Hackle

Tailwaters love it... probably taken probably as a caddis or midge

"JOHNNY FLASH"

Borrowed from Stephen... remember to return.

BRASSIE

Z-WING CADDIS PUPA

PRINCE

fatboad many Missouri River Bows with this one... not a bad eastern fly either

HARE'S EAR

a freestone favorite, the number one generally "buggy" favorite...

PHEASANT-TAIL

SKYFISHING

Words by Gideon Sterer
Pictures by Poly Bernatene

Abrams Books for Young Readers
New York

When we picked Grandpa up to come live with us in the city, he brought every one of his fishing poles.

He had been a fisherman his entire life, so it didn't take him long to realize that where we lived . . .

. . . there was nowhere to fish.

We tried new hobbies
that fall ...

and winter.

But for Grandpa, there was nothing that could take fishing's place.

So in spring we tried something else.
"Let's pretend," I said.

So we did.

And for a while our lines dangled empty . . .

but when the first fish bit, it didn't feel so pretend anymore . . .

and we weren't sure what to do.

"REEL IT IN!"

Grandpa said he'd never seen one
before, but there it was . . .

A Flying Litterfish.

"There are two rules to fishing," he told me.
"If you catch something, put it back,
and where there's one fish,
you can bet there will be more."

I'd never fished before, but already I was hooked.

The first day's haul
was impressive.

There were Green Danglers,

Chimefish,

and Signfish.

Laundry Eels

and even a Cold-air-square.

But none of them were fast swimmers, so they were easy
to catch. The bigger challenges waited further in the
deep, and would require patience, practice, and study.

Below us the sidewalk flowed slowly.
It was the perfect place to start.

Capfish were the first to bite.

then Songfish,

Then Mexican Capfish,

And as the days got warmer, new and exotic fishes visited from foreign shores.

and Goldfish.

We fished every day, reeling in Furry Snappers, Lovefins, and Hammerheads . . .

until, at last, we caught the sidewalk's biggest prize—the Grillfish—

and we knew we were ready for the road itself.

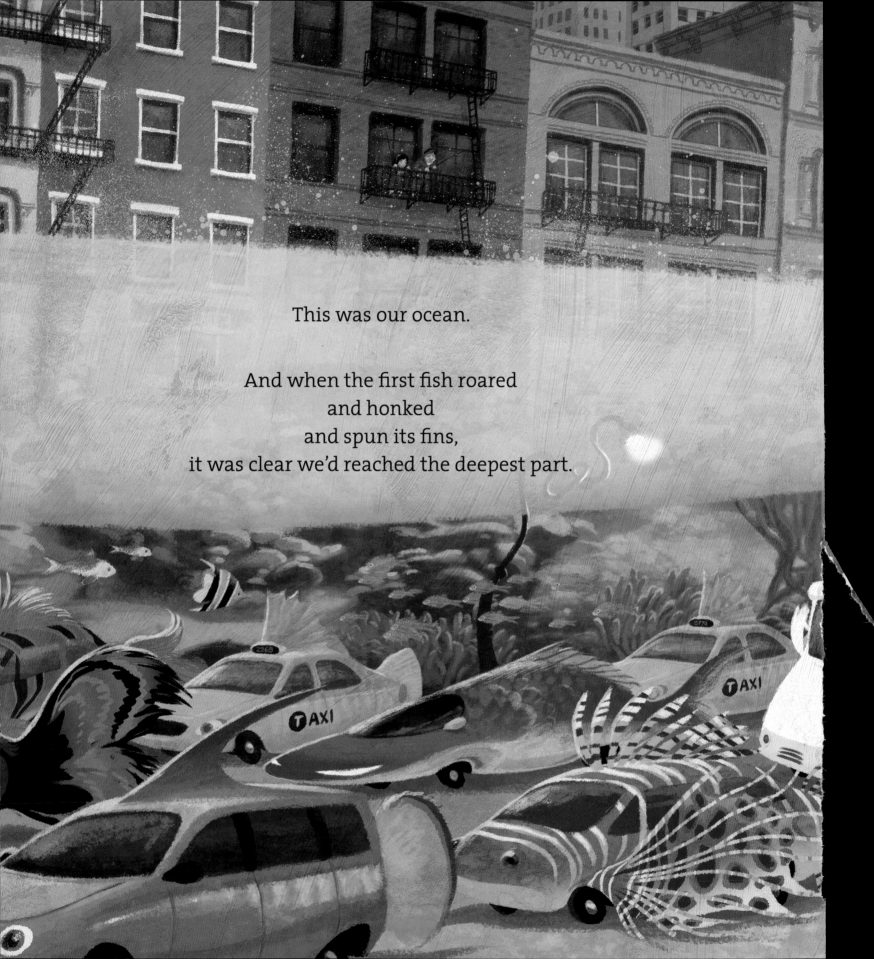

This was our ocean.

And when the first fish roared
and honked
and spun its fins,
it was clear we'd reached the deepest part.

There were Zoomfish, Mailfish, Glowfish,
and more Yellow-stripers than we could count.

But as big as they were, we knew they weren't the biggest.

The biggest wasn't a Stretchfish
or a Waste-muncher.
It wasn't a Constructionfish,
a Steeltail,
or even a Grouper.

For months we'd studied the
sidewalk and searched the streets.
We knew we'd seen it before,
but where?
We remembered from its rumble.
The biggest fish lived even deeper.
The biggest fish . . .

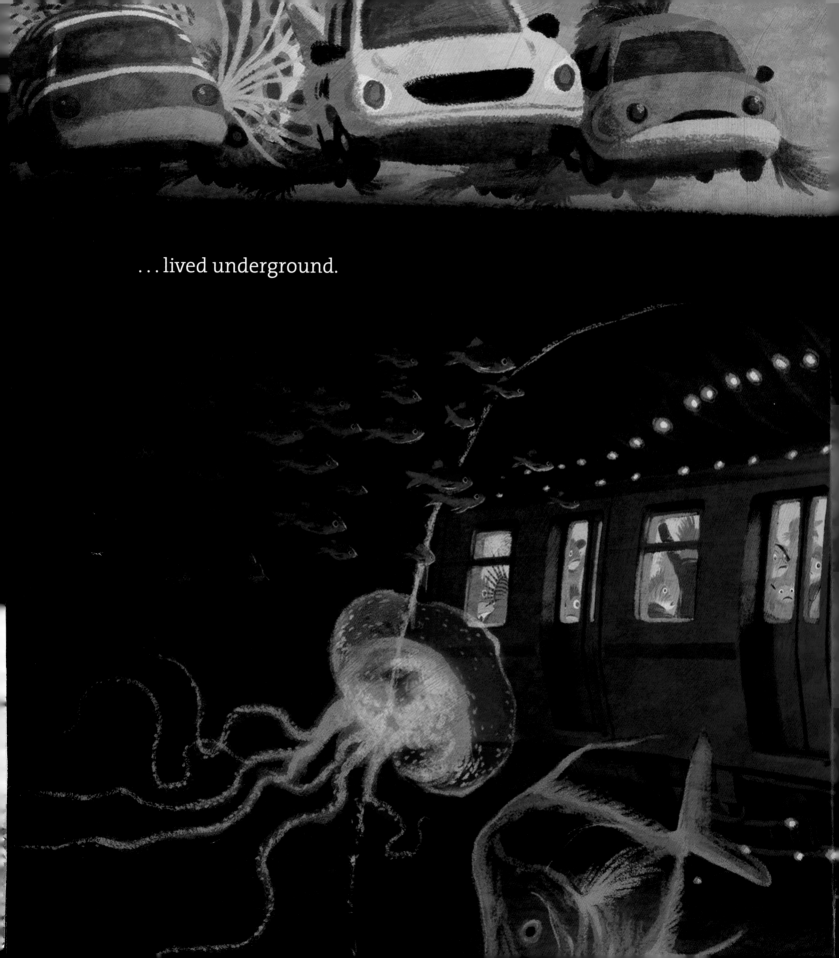

...lived underground.

But you can only hide for so long. So it was no surprise when at last we caught . . .

The Troublefish.

"Almost," I said to Grandpa.
"Almost," he said to me.

Then, in quiet, we packed our poles. The biggest fish would have to wait.

But things could have been worse.

Summer meant summer vacation,

and it was time to swim.

Library of Congress Cataloging-in-Publication Data Names: Sterer, Gideon, author. | Bernatene, Poly, illustrator. Title: Skyfishing / by Gideon Sterer ; illustrated by Poly Bernatene. Description: New York : Abrams Books for Young Readers, 2017. | Summary: "A young girl helps her grandfather adjust to his new home in the city with her family by inventing a fantastical fishing game"— Provided by publisher. Identifiers: LCCN 2016009639 | ISBN 9781419719110 Subjects: | CYAC: Grandparent and child—Fiction. | Grandfathers—Fiction. | Fishing—Fiction. | Imagination—Fiction. Classification: LCC PZ7.1.S74428 Sk 2017 | DDC [E]—dc23 LC record available at https://lccn.loc.gov/2016009639

ABRAMS The Art of Books
115 West 18th Street, New York, NY 10011
abramsbooks.com

Pursefish

TAXI

yellow-striper

CATFISH

Schooler

TURTLE CRAB

Tracktrout

Grouper

Firefish